What is precipitation?

Robin Johnson

Crabtree Publishing Company
www.crabtreebooks.com

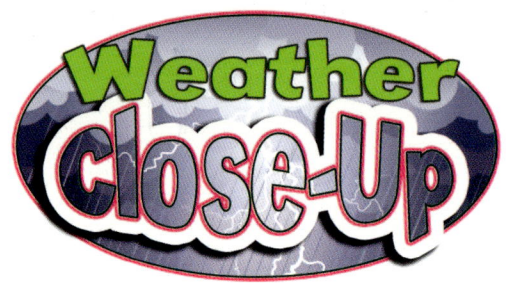

Author
Robin Johnson

Publishing plan research and development
Sean Charlebois, Reagan Miller
Crabtree Publishing Company

Editors
Reagan Miller, Crystal Sikkens

Proofreader
Kathy Middleton

Photo research
Crystal Sikkens

Design
Ken Wright

Production coordinator and prepress technician
Ken Wright

Print coordinator
Katherine Berti

Illustrations
Barbara Bedell: page 8
Katherine Berti: page 9

Photographs
David Saville/FEMA News Photo: page 14
Shutterstock: front cover, pages 4, 5, 6, 7, 11 (inset), 15, 17, 18 (except ruler), 20, 21
Thinkstock: back cover, pages 1, 3, 10, 11 (except inset), 12, 13 (bottom), 18 (ruler), 19, 22
Wikimedia Commons: Mike Epp: page 13 (top); NASA Kennedy Space Center: page 16

Library and Archives Canada Cataloguing in Publication

Johnson, Robin (Robin R.)
   What is precipitation? / Robin Johnson.

(Weather close-up)
Includes index.
Issued also in electronic formats.
ISBN 978-0-7787-0754-7 (bound).--ISBN 978-0-7787-0761-5 (pbk.)

   1. Precipitation (Meteorology)--Juvenile literature.
I. Title. II. Series: Weather close-up

QC920.J64 2012   j551.57'7   C2012-903947-0

Library of Congress Cataloging-in-Publication Data

CIP available at Library of Congress

Crabtree Publishing Company

www.crabtreebooks.com   1-800-387-7650

Printed in Hong Kong/092012/BK20120629

Copyright © **2013 CRABTREE PUBLISHING COMPANY**. All rights reserved. No part of this publication may be reproduced, stored in a retrieval system or be transmitted in any form or by any means, electronic, mechanical, photocopying, recording, or otherwise, without the prior written permission of Crabtree Publishing Company. In Canada: We acknowledge the financial support of the Government of Canada through the Canada Book Fund for our publishing activities.

Published in Canada
Crabtree Publishing
616 Welland Ave.
St. Catharines, Ontario
L2M 5V6

Published in the United States
Crabtree Publishing
PMB 59051
350 Fifth Avenue, 59th Floor
New York, New York 10118

Published in the United Kingdom
Crabtree Publishing
Maritime House
Basin Road North, Hove
BN41 1WR

Published in Australia
Crabtree Publishing
3 Charles Street
Coburg North
VIC 3058

Contents

What is precipitation? 4
We need rain! 6
The water cycle 8
Rain or snow?..................................10
Watch for falling ice!.......................12
When it rains, it pours! 14
Studying the sky 16
Make a rain gauge 18
Be a rain brain! 20
Graphing rain 22
Find out more 23
Glossary and Index.........................24

What is precipitation?

Precipitation is water that falls from clouds. Water falls down to Earth as rain. When it rains you can splash in puddles with your rubber boots. Water also falls to Earth as snow. It is fun to make snowmen and ride sleds when it snows! Rain, snow, **hail**, and **sleet** are all kinds of precipitation.

What do you think?

Snow is solid precipitation. How do you know that snow is solid?

Wet weather

Precipitation is part of the **weather**. Weather is what the air and sky are like each day. Precipitation, clouds, wind, and **temperature** all make up the weather. Weather changes from day to day and over the seasons. It can even change from hour to hour! Have you ever been outside when it suddenly started to rain?

Rain is liquid precipitation. It flows and drips down your umbrella.

We need rain!

All living things need water to grow and stay alive. Rain and snow give people and animals **fresh water** to drink. Rain goes into the soil and gives plants the water they need to grow. Precipitation also fills the lakes and rivers around the world.

In winter, some animals eat snow when they cannot find water to drink.

Water from many rivers and lakes is taken by pipes for use in our homes.

What do you think?

We use water to clean our bodies and wash our clothes. What else do we need water for?

The water cycle

Water is always moving from place to place. It falls down from the clouds as precipitation. Precipitation falls into lakes, rivers, and oceans. The Sun heats the water. Some of the water changes from a liquid to a gas called **water vapor**. This change from a liquid to a gas is called **evaporation**.

Up and down

Water vapor rises high in the sky. The gets colder as the vapor rises. The vapor starts to cool and turns into tiny droplets of water. This change from gas to liquid is called **condensation**. Many water droplets join together and form clouds. Water falls from the clouds as precipitation and the cycle starts over again.

The movement of water down to Earth and back up to the sky is called the water cycle.

Rain or snow?

What do you think?

Why do we get rain in the spring and snow in the winter?

The type of precipitation that falls from the clouds depends on the temperature of the air. Temperature is how hot or cold something is. When the air temperature is warm, water droplets fall from the clouds as rain.

Cold as ice

When the air temperature is very cold, water droplets in the clouds freeze and form **ice crystals**. Ice crystals are frozen drops of water. Ice crystals fall from the clouds as snow.

When ice crystals freeze they create snowflakes in all different shapes.

Watch for falling ice!

Rain and snow are not the only forms of precipitation. Hail, sleet, and freezing rain are other forms of precipitation that happen when it is cold. Freezing rain is rain that turns into ice when it touches the ground.

Freezing rain can cover trees, roads, cars, and homes with smooth, heavy ice.

Sleet is rain that turns into ice pellets as it falls from the clouds. Ice pellets are small, hard bits of ice that bounce when they hit the ground.

Hail is hard chunks or balls of ice that form inside clouds. Some chunks are as big as baseballs! Hail can cause a lot of damage when it lands on cars and buildings.

When it rains, it pours!

Floods can damage or wash away trees, roads, cars, and even houses!

Sometimes, a lot of precipitation falls in a short period of time. When too much rain falls, there may be **floods**. Floods can happen when rivers or lakes get too full and the water flows out over land that is usually dry. Floods can happen quickly, so it is best to stay away from rivers or lakes during heavy rainfalls.

Snowed in!

When a lot of snow falls in a short time, it is called a snowstorm. Snowstorms can bury roads, sidewalks, and cars under thick layers of snow. The snow makes it hard for people to get from place to place. Heavy snow can also damage buildings and trees.

Studying the sky

Meteorologists use weather satellites and other tools to predict rain and snow. Satellites are objects that take pictures of the air and clouds from space.

Meteorologists are scientists that study and measure weather. They use different tools to collect weather data, or information. They use this information to **predict** the weather that is coming. Meteorologists warn people when there is heavy rain or big snowstorms on the way.

Weather patterns

Meteorologists measure and record the amount of precipitation that falls in a set period of time. They study this data and look for weather patterns. A pattern is something that repeats over time. By studying weather patterns, meteorologists can use weather from the past to help predict the weather in the future.

Have you ever heard people say that April showers bring May flowers? In some places, rain in spring is a pattern that repeats each year.

Make a rain gauge

Meteorologists use tools called rain gauges to measure how much rain falls in a set period of time. A rain gauge is a clear container with lines on it marking inches or centimeters. When it rains, the water collects in the container and can be measured. Follow these steps to make your own rain gauge.

Materials:
scissors
plastic bottle
flower pot
tape
marker
ruler

What to do:

1. Remove the cap from the bottle. Ask a parent or other adult to help you cut off the top of the bottle.

2. Turn the top of the bottle upside down and tape it to the bottom of the bottle.

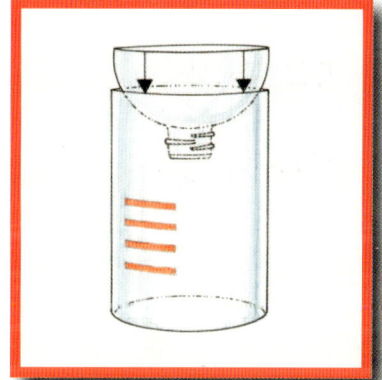

3. Use a ruler and a marker to make lines on the bottle that are 1/2 inch or one cm apart. Start at zero at the bottom.

4. Place the bottle outdoors inside a pot so the wind does not blow it over.

5. After it rains, the line the water level has reached is the amount it has rained.

Be a rain brain!

You can use your rain gauge to collect data about the weather around you. Check your rain gauge at the same time each day. Use the lines on the side of the bottle to measure the amount of precipitation. Record the measurements in a weather journal. A weather journal is a notebook for recording information about rain, snow, and other weather.

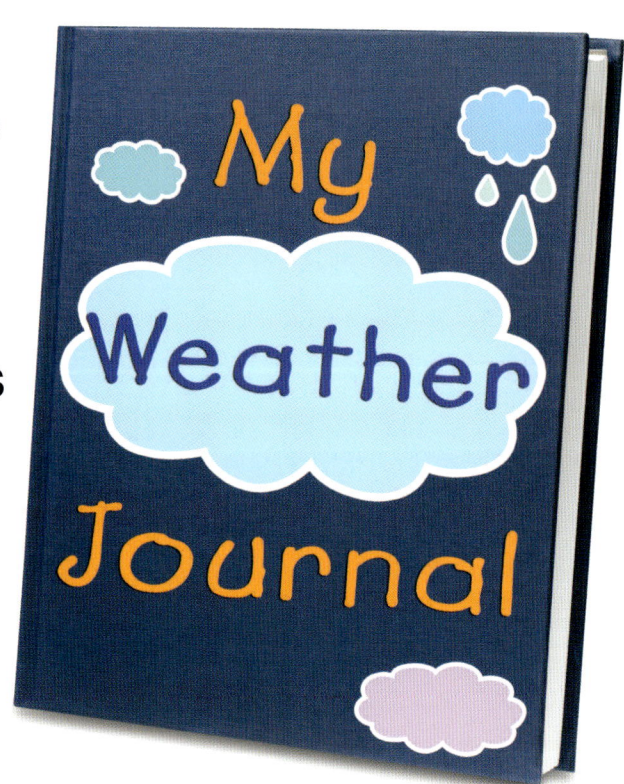

Explain the rain

Study your weather journal. Over time, you will begin to see weather patterns form. Does the rain usually fall in the morning or afternoon? Does it rain more in the spring or in the summer? How does the sky look right before it starts to rain? Soon you will be a real rain brain!

You can draw pictures in your journal to show how the weather looks each day.

Graphing rain

Where Cassie lives it rains almost every day in the summer. She recorded the daily rainfall for one week and created the graph below to display her data. Now, graph the rain data from your weather journal over several weeks. Compare the amount of rain from week to week.

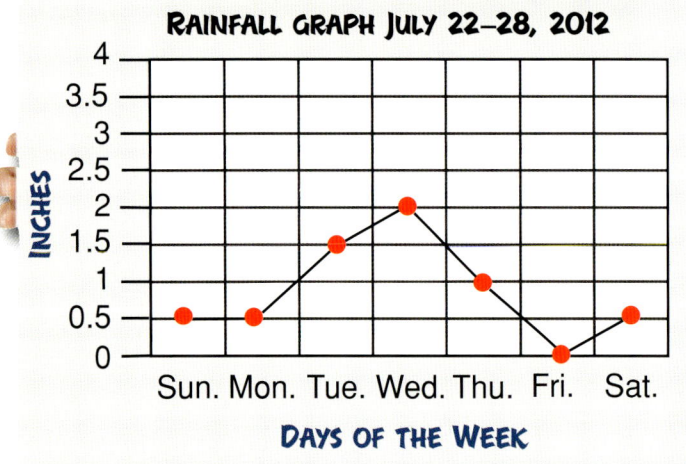

Look at Cassie's graph. What day of the week had the most rain? What day of the week would be best for outdoor activities?

Find out more

Books

Changing Weather: Storms by Kelley MacAulay and Bobbie Kalman. Crabtree Publishing Company, 2006.

It's Wet Out! by Kris Hirschmann. Checkerboard Books, 2008.

What is climate? (Big Science Ideas) by Bobbie Kalman. Crabtree Publishing Company, 2012.

Precipitation (Water Science) by Frances Purslow. Av2 by Weigl, 2010.

The Water Cycle by Bobbie Kalman and Rebecca Sjonger. Crabtree Publishing Company, 2006.

Websites

United States Search and Rescue Task Force: Predicting Weather
http://www.ussartf.org/predicting_weather.htm

Weather Wiz Kids
www.weatherwizkids.com

Glossary

Note: Some boldfaced words are defined where they appear in the book.

condensation (kon-den-SEY-shuhn) *noun* The change in form from gas to liquid

evaporation (ih-vap-uh-REY-shuhn) *noun* The change in form from liquid to gas

flood (fluhd) *noun* Water flowing onto land that is usually dry

fresh water (fresh WOT-er) *noun* Water that does not have a lot of salt and is good to drink

hail (HEYL) *noun* Hard chunks of ice that fall from the sky

ice crystals (ahys KRIS-tls) *noun* Small pieces of ice that form in the clouds when the air is cold

predict (pri-DIKT) *verb* To tell something before it takes place

sleet *noun* A mix of liquid and solid water that falls as ice pellets

temperature (TEHM-per-a-chur) *noun* How cold or warm the air is

water vapor (WOT-er VEY-per) *noun* Water in the form of gas that you cannot see

A noun is a person, place, or thing. A verb is an action word that tells you what someone or something does.

Index

clouds 4, 5, 8, 10, 11, 13, 16
floods 14
ice 11, 12–13

meteorologists 16–17
rain 4, 5, 6, 10, 12, 13, 14, 16, 17, 18–19, 20, 21, 22

snow 4, 6, 11, 12, 15, 16, 20
temperature 5, 10, 11
tools 16, 18–19